The TWELVE DAYS OF CHRISTMAS

Illustrated by
Susan Swan

Troll Associates

Library of Congress Cataloging in Publication Data

Twelve days of Christmas (English folk song)
   The twelve days of Christmas.

   SUMMARY: More and more gifts arrive from a
young girl's true love on each of the 12 days of
Christmas.
   1. Folk-songs, English—Texts.   2. Christmas
music.   [1. Folk songs, English.   2. Christmas
music]   I. Swan, Susan Elizabeth.
PZ8.3.T8517Sw   784.6'8394268282   80-28097
ISBN 0-89375-474-9
ISBN 0-89375-475-7 (pbk.)

The TWELVE DAYS OF CHRISTMAS

On the first day of Christmas,
my true love sent to me

a partridge in a pear tree.

On the second day of Christmas,
my true love sent to me
two turtledoves,
and a partridge in a pear tree.

On the third day of Christmas,
my true love sent to me
three French hens,

two turtledoves,
and a partridge in a pear tree.

On the fourth day of Christmas,
my true love sent to me
four calling birds,

three French hens,
two turtledoves,
and a partridge in a pear tree.

On the fifth day of Christmas,
my true love sent to me
five gold rings,

four calling birds,
three French hens,
two turtledoves,
and a partridge in a pear tree.

On the sixth day of Christmas,
my true love sent to me
six geese a-laying,
five gold rings,
four calling birds,
three French hens,
two turtledoves,
and a partridge in a pear tree.

On the seventh day of Christmas,
my true love sent to me
seven swans a-swimming,

six geese a-laying,
five gold rings,
four calling birds,
three French hens,
two turtledoves,
and a partridge in a pear tree.

On the eighth day of Christmas,
my true love sent to me
eight maids a-milking,
seven swans a-swimming,
six geese a-laying,

five gold rings,
four calling birds,
three French hens,
two turtledoves,
and a partridge in a pear tree.

On the ninth day of Christmas,
my true love sent to me
nine ladies dancing,
eight maids a-milking,
seven swans a-swimming,
six geese a-laying,
five gold rings,
four calling birds,
three French hens,
two turtledoves,
and a partridge in a pear tree.

On the tenth day of Christmas,
my true love sent to me
ten lords a-leaping,

nine ladies dancing,
eight maids a-milking,
seven swans a-swimming,

six geese a-laying,
five gold rings,
four calling birds,
three French hens,
two turtledoves,
and a partridge in a pear tree.

On the eleventh day of Christmas,
my true love sent to me
eleven pipers piping,

ten lords a-leaping,
nine ladies dancing,
eight maids a-milking,
seven swans a-swimming,
six geese a-laying,
five gold rings,
four calling birds,

three French hens,

two turtledoves,

and a partridge in a pear tree.

On the twelfth day of Christmas,
my true love sent to me
twelve drummers drumming,

eleven pipers piping,
ten lords a-leaping,
nine ladies dancing,

eight maids a-milking,
seven swans a-swimming,
six geese a-laying,
five gold rings,
four calling birds,
three French hens,
two turtledoves,

and a partridge in a pear tree.